MW00965658

SHORT TALES
Furlock & Muttson Mysteries

The case of
THE Community GARDEN

by Robin Koontz

visit us at www.abdopublishing.com

Printed in the United States of America, North Mankato, Minnesota.
092009
012010

 PRINTED ON RECYCLED PAPER

Written and illustrated by Robin Koontz
Edited by Stephanie Hedlund and Rochelle Baltzer
Interior Layout by Kristen Fitzner Denton
Book Design and Packaging by Shannon Eric Denton

Library of Congress Cataloging-in-Publication Data

Koontz, Robin Michal.
   The case of the community garden / written and illustrated by Robin Koontz.
      p. cm. -- (Short tales. Furlock & Muttson mysteries)
   ISBN 978-1-60270-558-6
   [1. Gardening--Fiction. 2. Mystery and detective stories.] I. Title.
   PZ7.K83574Cas 2010
   [E]--dc22
                                                        2008032514

"Muttson, why are you pouring water on the
ground?" asked Furlock.
"I am watering my tomato plants," said Muttson.
"I planted the seeds last month."

"Soon we will have fresh tomatoes,"
said Muttson.
"Yum!" said Furlock.

"Hello!" a voice called.
Mrs. Bloom waved from across the street.
"Can you please help me?" she asked.
"We are on our way!" called Furlock.

"What can we do for you?" Furlock asked.
"We need help at our community garden,"
said Mrs. Bloom. "Things are missing!"

Furlock and Muttson drove Mrs. Bloom to the community garden.
"What is that bright light?" asked Muttson.
"That is coming from Mr. Skunk's garage," said Mrs. Bloom.

"Everyone, meet Furlock and Muttson,
private detectives!" she said.
Muttson took out his notepad.
"What is missing?" asked Furlock.

"Our tomato plants are missing," said one gardener.

"Our corn plants are missing," said another gardener.

"Our bean plants are also missing," said a third gardener.

"What do the plants look like?" asked Furlock.
"They are green," said Mrs. Bloom.
"Interesting," said Furlock.

"Muttson, please check for footprints."
"I see footprints here," said Muttson.
They followed the footprints to a shed.

"What is in this shed?" asked Muttson.
"Garden tools," said Mrs. Bloom. "We share them
with anyone who needs them."

Furlock peeked inside.
"Where is the light?" she asked.
"Oh dear!" said Mrs. Bloom. "The light is missing, too!"

"The footprints lead behind the shed,"
said Muttson.
They walked behind the shed.

"There is a hole here," said Muttson.
He peeked inside the hole.
"It looks like a gopher hole."
"Gophers do like garden plants," said Mrs. Bloom.

"We have our thief!" said Furlock.
"Oh dear!" said Mrs. Bloom. "That is very
bad news for our community garden."

"There is light in the hole," said Muttson.
He grabbed a hose and fed it into the hole.
"Hello in there!" he called.

Suddenly the hose disappeared.
"Hey!" cried Muttson.
"Stop, thief!" Furlock cried into the hole.
There was no answer.

"Let me try," said Mrs. Bloom.
"This is Mrs. Bloom," she said into the hole.
"Please come over, Mrs. Bloom," said a voice.
They all raced next door.

Mr. Skunk greeted them at the gate.
"Hello, everyone!" he said.
"Ew!" cried the gardeners. They held their
noses.
"Oh well," said Mr. Skunk. He ran to his
house.

"Wait! Where are the missing plants?"
cried Furlock.

"I found them," said Muttson.
"They are inside Mr. Skunk's garage."
They went inside the garage.

Inside, tables had trays of water.
The plants were in pots in the trays.
"There is the light from the shed!" Furlock cried.

"It is nice and warm in here," said Mrs. Bloom.
"The plants all look good," said Muttson.
Mr. Skunk peeked through the door.

"Why did you do this?" asked Furlock.
"There is a freeze coming," said Mr. Skunk.
"A freeze in April?" asked Mrs. Bloom.

"I tried to warn you, but you all ran away,"
said Mr. Skunk.
"Well, you are a skunk after all," said Mrs. Bloom.
"I only stink when I am scared," said Mr. Skunk.

"This is a very nice plant house," said Muttson.
"Thank you," said Mr. Skunk. "The trays of
water keep the plants wet. The light helps the
plants grow."

"What about the hole?" asked Furlock.
"The hole is for fresh air," said Mr. Skunk.
"And it doesn't let out the heat."

"Let's leave the plants here," said the gardeners.
"I agree," said Mrs. Bloom.
"Have some of my homemade zucchini cookies,"
said Mr. Skunk.

"Thank you!" said Furlock.
They all grabbed a zucchini cookie.
"Muththon, on thoo thuh neth caseth!" cried
Furlock.
"I am right behind you," said Muttson.

They jumped into the Furlock-Mobile
and sped away.